A Taste of Honey

Written and illustrated by

Nancy Elizabeth Wallace

Marshall Cavendish

New York London Singapore

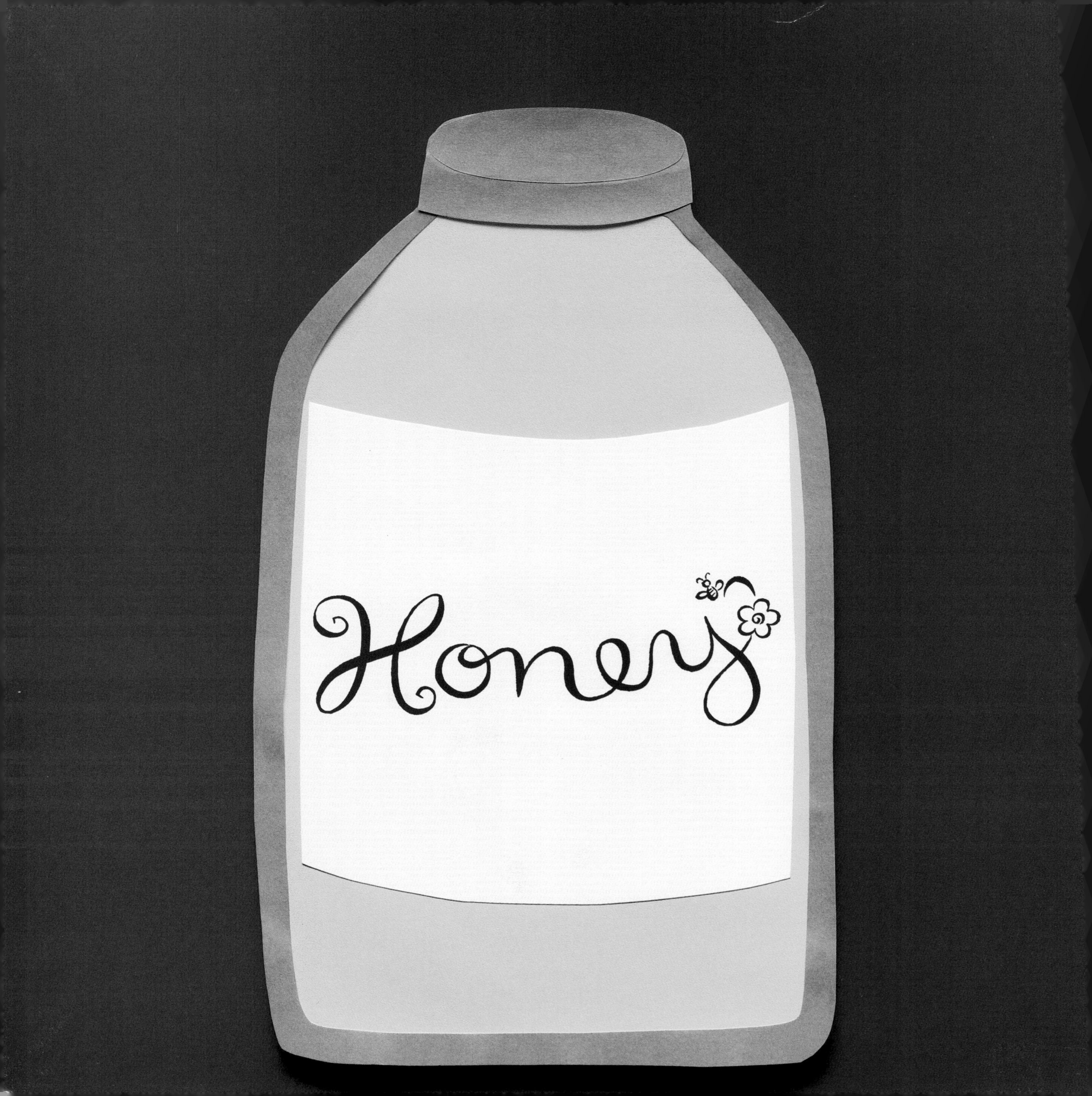
Honey

"H-O-N-E-Y," Lily read.

She opened the jar.

She looked.

She sniffed.

She touched.

Then she asked Poppy some questions.

"Poppy?"

"Yes, Lily."

"Where does honey come from?"

"Well, we just spooned it out of this jar."

"But...
before
that?"

"I bought this honey at Mike's Market."

"A truck drove it to Mike's."

"Before that?"

North America

South America

Honey comes from every continent except Antarctica.

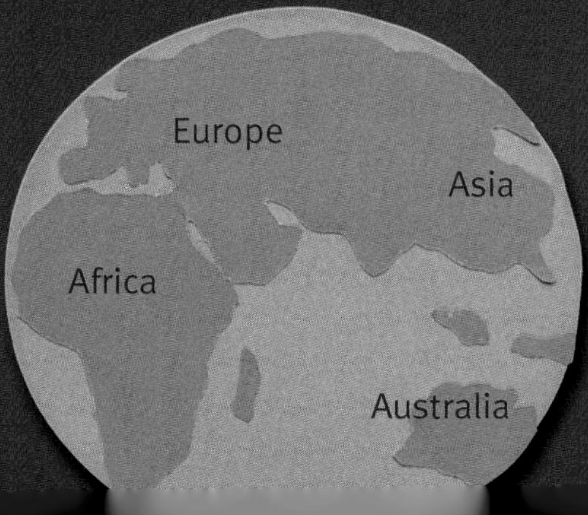

Europe

Asia

Africa

Australia

"It came from a honey farm."

Honey
House
(where honey is made
ready for the market)

"Before that?"

AMY'S
APiARY
a honey of a farm

"It was whirled around and around in a honey extractor."

"And...

Extractor

Honeycombs are put into an extractor. Then they are whirled around and around very fast.

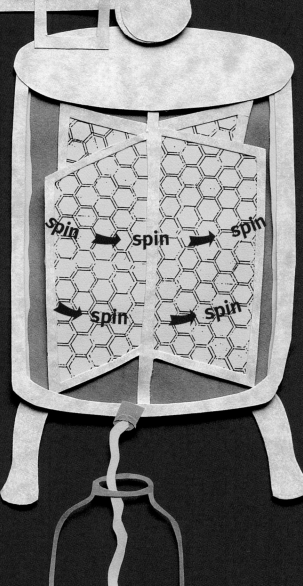

Turn the crank.

Honey flies out to the sides and drips down.

spin → spin → spin

spin → spin

Honey comes out through a spout.

before that?"

JAR
LABELS

Honey

"The honey was uncapped."

The warm knife blade melts the wax cap from each cell, so the honey can flow free.

wood handle

warm knife blade

electric heated knife

"Before that?"

Blossom

P.T.

JOE

The prongs pierce the wax.

cappings scratcher

"A beekeeper collected it at harvest time."

Clothing for Beekeepers

Beekeepers wear special clothing to protect them from being stung.

helmet

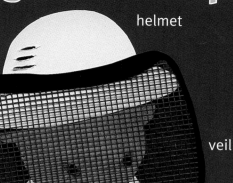

veil

AmY

"Before that?"

Sting resistant gloves and elastic cuffs or boot bands are worn to keep **bees** from flying up the pants.

White coveralls are worn because dark colors make **bees** more aggressive.

boots

"It was stored in a hive."

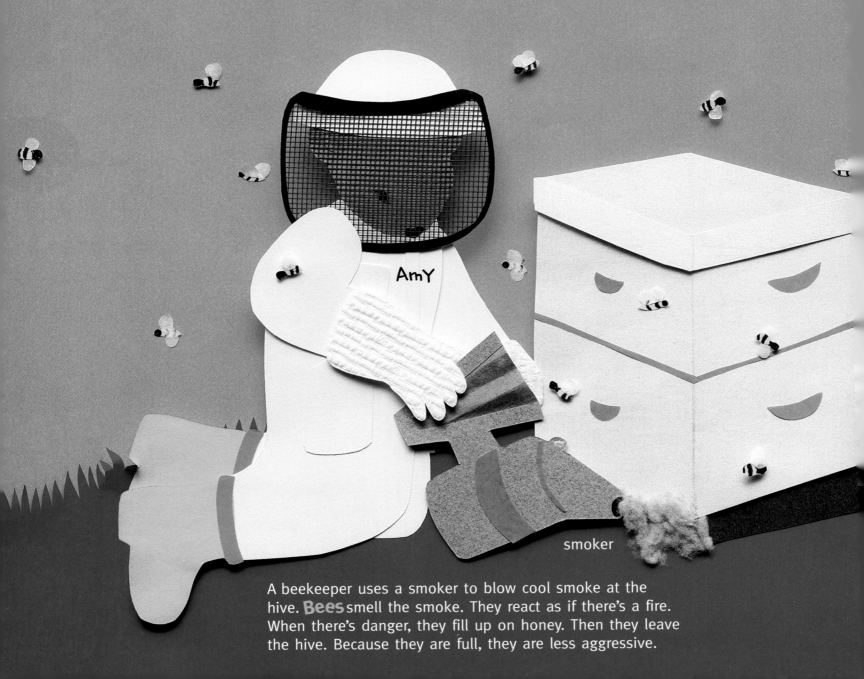

A beekeeper uses a smoker to blow cool smoke at the
hive. Bees smell the smoke. They react as if there's a fire.
When there's danger, they fill up on honey. Then they leave
the hive. Because they are full, they are less aggressive.

A frame grip is used to lift the frames.

JOE

A bee brush is used to remove **bees** from frames and clothes without hurting them.

Bellows blow the smoke.

"Before that?"

"It filled a honeycomb."

A wax cell is shaped like a hexagon.

A hexagon has six sides.

1
6   2
5   3
4

The cells are tilted slightly up,

so the honey does not run out.

"Before that?"

wildflowers

Nectar is the sweet liquid in many flowers. **Honey** will look and taste different depending on what flowers the nectar comes from.

buckwheat

alfalfa

"The sweet nectar of flowers was gathered to make it."

"But, Poppy, what was there before the nectar?"

"I've run out of ideas, Lily."

clover

manuka

tupelo

orange blossom

zzzzzzzzzzzzzzzzzzzzzzzzzzz bbbbbbbbbbbbbbbbbbzzzzzzzzzzzzzzz

zzzzzzzzzzzzz

zzzz

"I know," said Lily.

"Bees,

Poppy!"

zzz

zzzzzzzzzzzzzzzzzzzzz

zzzz

zzz

ZZZZZZZZ

ZZ

ZZZZZZZZZZZ

How Worker Bees Make Honey

Worker honeybees are all females. A worker can "tell" other worker **bees** where nectar is with a special dance.

She does a **round dance** if the nectar is nearby.

She does a **wagging dance** if the nectar is farther away.

A worker honeybee drinks nectar through her long tongue, called a proboscis. It is like a drinking straw.

Honeybees have a special extra stomach for making **honey**. In the "honey stomach," nectar from flowers mixes with enzymes to make **honey**.

It takes about 1,000 flower visits to fill a honeybee's stomach, which is about the size of a grain of rice.

Worker **bees** also build the wax honeycombs.

"Poppy?"
"Yes, Lily."

"Where does bread come from?"

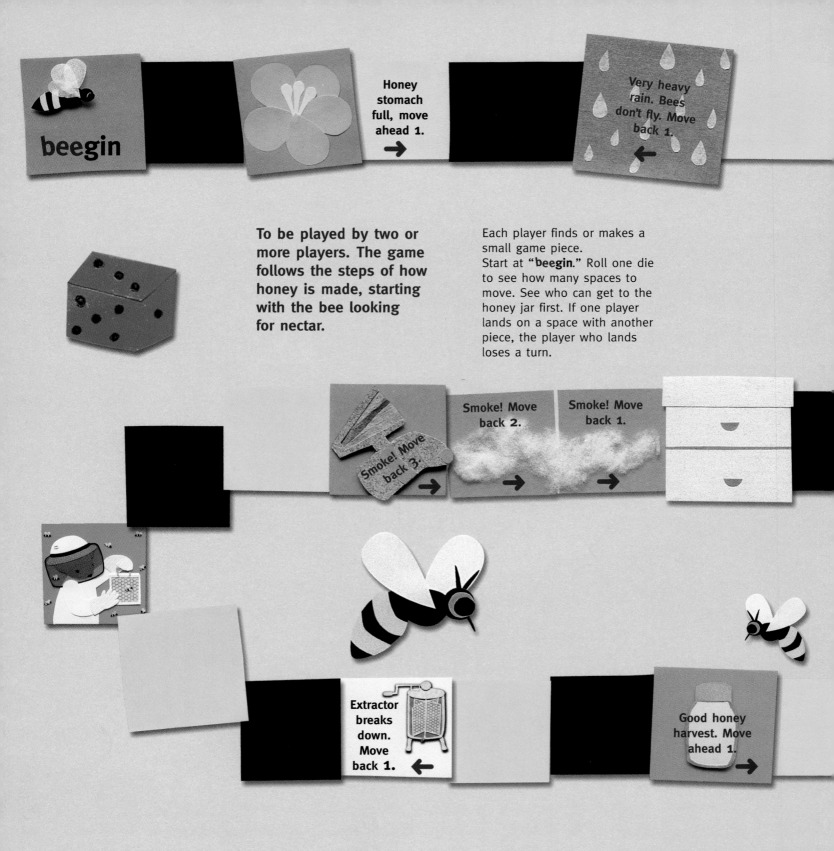

beegin

Honey stomach full, move ahead 1. ➡

Very heavy rain. Bees don't fly. Move back 1. ⬅

To be played by two or more players. The game follows the steps of how honey is made, starting with the bee looking for nectar.

Each player finds or makes a small game piece.
Start at **"beegin."** Roll one die to see how many spaces to move. See who can get to the honey jar first. If one player lands on a space with another piece, the player who lands loses a turn.

Smoke! Move back 3. ➡

Smoke! Move back 2. ➡

Smoke! Move back 1. ➡

Extractor breaks down. Move back 1. ⬅

Good honey harvest. Move ahead 1. ➡

honey game

Too windy to fly. Move back 2. ←

Bees don't fly at night. Move back 1. ←

Warm sunny day. Move ahead 1. →

Stuck in the honeycomb. Miss 1 turn.

Grass, no flowers. Move back 1. →

Field of clover. Move ahead 1.

Temperature below 45 degrees. Too cold for bees. Move back 1. →

You need to roll the exact number to reach the end.

Flat tire. Move back 1. ←

Big order from Mike's Market. Move ahead 2. →

Honey sold out. Move back 2. ←

a sweet treat
Honey

Honey Facts

Apis mellifera is the Latin word for a honeybee.

Apis means bee; **mellifera** means honey bearer.

The record for the most honey harvested from a single hive is 404 pounds.

Bees are not the only insects that produce honey.

Little sucking insects called aphids secrete "honeydew."

Honey is heavy. A pint weighs one-and-a-half pounds. A pint of water weighs one pound.

Honey is an excellent energy food. There are 65 calories in a tablespoon of honey. There are 48 calories in a tablespoon of sugar.

The word honey is spoken in many languages. Here are a few:

Japanese–hachimítsu, **Swahili**–asali, **Russian**–myot, **Turkish**–bal, **Indonesian**–mada

Saying: You can catch more flies with honey than you can with vinegar!

To my mom, Alexine; Auntie Lib; cousin Barbara; niece Amy;
and husband, Peter. Also to the memory of
Aunt Bea and my dad, Jack, aka Poppy
Love you.
–N.E.W.

Special thanks to Carol R. Lemmon,
deputy state entomologist for Connecticut;
Phil Higgins, beekeeper; Roger and Romi at K&G Graphics;
Barbara, Catherine, and Deb, Reference Librarians,
Blackstone Library; and Carole Crysler

Text and illustration copyright © 2001 by Nancy Elizabeth Wallace

All rights reserved
Marshall Cavendish, 99 White Plains Road, Tarrytown, NY, 10591
www.marshallcavendish.us

Library of Congress Cataloging-in-Publication Data

Wallace, Nancy Elizabeth.
A taste of honey / written and illustrated by Nancy Elizabeth Wallace.— 1st
Marshall Cavendish paperback ed.
p. cm.
Summary: A little bear and her father trace the origins of honey from
the jar all the way back to the bees that first produced it.
ISBN 0–7614–5215–X
[1. Honey—Fiction. 2. Bears—Fiction.] I. Title.

PZ7.W15875Tas 2004
[E]—dc22
2003022115

The illustrations in this book were prepared with cut paper.
Creative Director: Bretton Clark
Designer: Victoria Stehl
Editor: Margery Cuyler

Printed in Malaysia
First Marshall Cavendish paperback edition, 2005
Reprinted by arrangement with
WinslowHouse International, Inc.

2 4 6 8 10 9 7 5 3 1

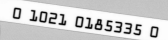